HIGH SPEED
SILENCE

HIGH SPEED
SILENCE

ALEX WADE

authorHOUSE®

AuthorHouse™
1663 Liberty Drive
Bloomington, IN 47403
www.authorhouse.com
Phone: 1-800-839-8640

First published by AuthorHouse   12/15/2011

ISBN: 978-1-4634-1553-2 (sc)
ISBN: 978-1-4567-9771-3 (ebk)

Library of Congress Control Number: 2011917509

Printed in the United States of America

Any people depicted in stock imagery provided by Thinkstock are models, and such images are being used for illustrative purposes only. Certain stock imagery © Thinkstock.

This book is printed on acid-free paper.

Because of the dynamic nature of the Internet, any web addresses or links contained in this book may have changed since publication and may no longer be valid. The views expressed in this work are solely those of the author and do not necessarily reflect the views of the publisher, and the publisher hereby disclaims any responsibility for them.

PROLOGUE

AN OLD JUNKIE DRESSED IN military fatigues and a red beret defecates by a drainpipe in a decrepit waterfront alley. Hastily wiping himself with ragged scraps of a brown paper bag, the wretch quicksteps away to distance himself from his freshly squeezed contribution to society.

Turning the corner, he bumps into an old pal from the neighborhood whom he hasn't seen in a while. His young friend appears to have cleaned himself up. "Hey, Johnny. Where the fuck you been?" the wretch greets him rudely. "Forgot about your old pal?"

"I'm clean now," the young man replies.

"Shi-i-t," the old bird sneers.

"I got a job and everything."

"What'd you go and do *that* for?" the old junkie spits. "Now you're just a cog in somebody else's wheel!"

"Everybody's got to learn sometime, I guess."

"Fuck that," the old bird cuts Johnny off. He's heard enough of his friend's success story. "Let's get high."

"Can't do it, bro. My probation officer drug tests me randomly. And besides, my old lady would *kill* me."

"Just this one last time, bro." The old junkie flashes the dopey grin he knows his friend can't resist. He remembers just the right buttons to push.

"All right, but just this once."

The temptation is just too great. Reluctantly, he hands over his cash, along with his hard-won salvation.

The old bird wastes no time. He darts around the corner to score, planning how he'll skim a little extra from his buddy's share along the way. *Serves him right for getting all uppity*, he thinks.

The old man steps up to a heavily tattooed thug with an eager expression.

"Step off, scumbag!" the thug says, waving him off. "Your money's no good here."

"Come on, bro." The old man waves a twenty under his nose. "Don't do me like that!"

"You hard of hearing, pal?" The dealer shoves him to the pavement and steps on his neck. "If you come around here again, I'll squash you like a bug!"

"Be cool! Be cool!" the junkie says, rolling over on his back. But instead of crawling off peacefully, he turns and spits at the dealer's feet. Big mistake.

The enraged dealer pursues him at full tilt, fully intent on restoring his street credibility.

"Break camp!" the old wretch warns his awaiting friend as he flies back around the corner. Together they hustle down the alley and duck into an abandoned row house. The enraged dealer is right on their heels and catches a glimpse of the old bird going out the bathroom window.

High Speed Silence

His young friend tries to dart out the front door, but the dealer plunges a knife into the young man's back before he can get very far. The last thing the young man remembers is the feel of the drug dealer's boot kicking him in the ribs to make sure he isn't faking.

The old bird is already long gone, having vanished like a cockroach into the dark crevices of the waterfront.

CHAPTER ONE

IN THE HEART OF EVERY city lies a bastion of worldly justice, a castle of decency amid a siege of bad behavior.

The north coast of California is known for its foggy weather. During summer a thick gray layer usually moves onshore in the early afternoon, snuffing out the warm, golden rays of the morning sun. There is a distinct change in mood as the accompanying temperature drops, turning an innocent day dark and foreboding. The most notorious police shooting in North Coast history took place on just such a day.

It happened on Highway 101 just outside Humboldt City on a sunny Fourth of July. Holiday traffic had come to a complete standstill on the freeway because of a fender bender. Irritated by the delay, frustrated drivers got out of their cars to see what was going on. Fifteen minutes later, no one had moved an inch. Worse yet, there was no sign of law enforcement or emergency personnel anywhere.

Lester, a grumpy old curmudgeon in an RV, finally reached his boiling point. He was already late for his weekly bingo game at the casino. Sweat stung his eyes. He brushed it away and then banged his fist on the AC panel. He'd paid fifty thousand dollars for this piece of crap RV, and now the air wasn't working. He glanced out the window at the wall of traffic that had ground to a halt. Where the hell are the police when you needed them? If he didn't get his vehicle rolling soon and get some fresh air blowing through the windows, he'd broil alive. Lester glanced over to the shoulder. It sat empty all the way to the Humboldt City exit, five hundred feet ahead. It seemed a bit narrow, but he felt sure that he could make it. Lester turned the wheel and pressed on the gas. His RV lurched out of line and onto the shoulder, sending dirt billowing up in clouds. He pushed forward a good two hundred feet and then noticed some young punk step out of an old El Camino and onto the shoulder. Lester slammed on the brakes and blared the horn, but the punk just flipped him the bird.

The young hooligan's hair was shaved up on one side, and long earrings dangled from both ears. Lester scowled. Only faggots wore earrings.

Lester blared the horn again. The punk ignored him, chugging down the last of a forty-ounce malt liquor and tossing the bottle into the ditch. *Goddamned litterbug,* Lester thought. *These kids have no respect for the law.* Lester honked again. The punk took a step, staggered a bit, and then assumed a steadier stance. With legs spread wide, the punk reached down, unzipped his pants, and pulled out his jimmy. Lester couldn't believe what he was seeing. For God's sake, there were women and children around. Lester honked the horn again, and again the punk shot him the bird. The punk proceeded to pee right on the side of the road. The urine struck the ground and spattered back on the kid's legs, but he didn't seem to notice.

Lester watched, flabbergasted. Sweat again stung his eyes, and he had to brush it out with his hands. He looked up and spotted a young girl in a pink sundress skipping between the cars with a sparkler in her hand. The girl approached the punk and slid to a halt. She stared for a moment. The punk spotted her and turned to wave. His jimmy stood in full view, splashing urine all over the road. The girl giggled and then ran off.

That was the last straw. Lester held down the horn and pressed the accelerator.

The young punk turned to look.

The RV bore down on him, but the punk refused to move. He just flashed Lester a sneer.

A sneer? Why, that bastard. Lester decided to scare the crap out of him. He refused to ease up on the accelerator until he was nearly on the kid, and then he slammed on the brakes. Unfortunately, the AC wasn't the only thing that didn't work right on this piece of shit RV. It slammed into the punk and slid a dozen feet past where Lester thought it would stop, dragging the kid the entire way.

The foolhardy youth evidently had not spent any time around grumpy old men. Lester was still spewing venom from his window when the frenzied crowd dragged him from his vehicle. Two of the victim's buddies started beating Lester to a pulp, just as the fog rolled in. Someone in the crowd tossed red smoke grenades onto the roadway, while others shot bottle rockets and tossed beer bottles into the melee.

Luckily, help was on the way. Knifing through the gridlock at high speed, silently weaving past pedestrians, motorcycle patrolman Adam King arrived at the scene. In one fluid motion, he dismounted his bike and sprinted toward the center of the action, simultaneously relaying information through his microphone headset. Without breaking stride, he pounced on the two young men beating up on Lester and yanked them both off by their hair. Outraged by such rough treatment, the two decided to gang up on the patrolman instead of surrendering. King knew he was in for a fight. The steely cop stood his ground as they began circling him like wolves. "It only gets worse from here," King said, warning them to back off. But the two had no intention of giving up peacefully. The one on the left, a wiry white boy in a wife-beater tank top with multiple piercings on his face, lunged forward. King neatly sidestepped him, tripping him at the ankles. The poor lad hurtled headlong into a parked car. The thud was sickening. He wobbled to his feet, blood streaming down his face from the collision. A torn eyebrow flapped open and hung down over his eye. The second stooge, a steroid-swollen gang banger with thick gold chains around his neck, was close behind. King spun deftly on his heels and launched a pulverizing heel kick to the meathead's groin. The big oaf buckled and groaned as he fell to his knees on the pavement. King then drew his Taser and issued an unmistakable warning in a loud clear voice:

"The next one of you who tries to put his hands on me *will be tasered*!"

Fueled by a volatile mixture of testosterone and crank, the wild-eyed thug unsheathed a belt-buckle knife and took a violent swipe at the patrolman's neck. King fired his Taser, but one of the copper wires got tangled and snapped, rendering it useless. "Ha!" the young thug laughed, and he resumed a fighting stance with the buckle knife. It was clear to King that this guy had done some training and probably would go for a kill shot if given the chance. King finally pulled his gun. "Last chance to *not* do something stupid . . ." he said coyly.

"Fat chance, pig!" the foolhardy youth snarled. In his twisted mind, he was fighting the system and the authority figures he despised. In reality, he'd simply brought a knife to a gunfight.

The stiff crack of the patrolman's Glock 22 cut through the air and delivered its message with lethal force. The recipient grimaced and then went slack, dropping to the pavement with an expression of disbelief on his face.

Most of the crowd fled in mass panic, terrified by the sight of a real shooting. It's not the same as it is on television. The moaning, massive pooling of blood, and involuntary twitching of the victim as the life runs out him are hard for even the most jaded veterans to witness. It's the kind of thing that changes you forever. The only person who stood his ground is the victim's buddy. The patrolman saw the shock and rage welling up in his eyes and knew what would come next.

"Double or nothing?" King said, coldly fixing his laser sights on the big oaf's chest. The words sounded like a brazen challenge at the time, but the streetwise officer knew it was the most effective way to discourage an assault. The hefty gang banger looked down at the bright red dot on his chest and put his hands up in surrender.

When backup officers arrived, they found King calmly directing traffic. A flood of law enforcement personnel descended upon the scene. The local news media were there in full force, eager to get the scoop of the year.

Leaning against his motorcycle with arms folded and calmly smoking a cigarette, the patrolman appeared oddly detached in the center of the storm. A beam of sunlight broke through the cloud cover, illuminating him briefly as though he were on a separate plane of existence. Although small in stature, he was tightly muscled and well-proportioned, and he moved with an extreme economy of motion. Decades of hard riding had sculpted him into a lean, mean machine. Everything about him suggested speed and toughness . . . like a bullet.

Lieutenant Dave Sharp was the supervisory officer on scene. Clad in a plain black Hugo Boss suit with a gold badge glinting on his waistband, he carried himself with the stony gravitas of a seasoned veteran. The tall, angular veteran listened grim faced as the patrolman described the sequence of events that led to the shooting. "He left me no choice," King explained. As the words left his mouth, the realization suddenly struck him that he had just shot someone. "So what happens next?" he asked.

"Sounds like a righteous shoot," Sharp reassured him. "But we do this by the book. Surrender your service weapon to the evidence tech, and meet me in my office ASAP."

King unloaded his weapon, just like he had been taught at the academy, and handed it over to the lieutenant. He felt like he had just lost his right arm.

As the lieutenant sped off in a dark sedan, Officer King took a final drag from his cigarette and then crushed it under his boot heel with a decisive twist. *How did I get here?* he asked himself. *All I ever wanted was to ride a motorcycle.*

*   *   *

The Humboldt City Courthouse is a five-story pink stucco building smack in the center of town. The drab concrete edifice is largely nondescript except for the weathered State of California shield above the front entrance. The county jail, nicknamed the Humboldt Hilton by locals, conjoins its north wall. The Humboldt City Police Department occupies the ground floor. Law enforcement vehicles buzz in and out of the underground parking garage like wasps from a nest.

A large group of protesters has already assembled on the front lawn of the courthouse. Angry citizens circle the block waving picket signs, chanting anti-police epithets, when Officer King arrives. He has to push his way to the garage ramp through a gauntlet of cameras and reporters and is safe only after the steel garage gate closes behind him. "Holy crap," he says to himself after dismounting his bike. "That didn't take long."

King knew exactly why they had assembled so quickly. A few months earlier, a local teenager had been shot and killed while trying to run from the police. The public protests went on for weeks. In the end, the officer was acquitted, which created even more public mistrust. It was a vicious cycle, and this new incident couldn't have come at a worse time.

King follows a long corridor and then takes the back stairs to the office. The walls are lined with portraits of fallen officers. "Hey, Swaggs," he says to the faded photo of Sergeant Steve Swaggart, his old partner. "Hope you're having fun in Margaritaville." The man in the photo has a broad, friendly face and a thick brown mustache. They had gone through everything together—the academy, field training, and the mandatory first year of probation. At different times, it looked like neither one of them was going to make it. King nearly quit when the department reneged on its promise to assign him a motorcycle officer slot, and Swaggs totaled four patrol cars in his first six months. The only way they got through it all was by spending their off-duty hours partying at a local pub wearing loud Hawaiian shirts. Swaggs always played *Margaritaville* on the jukebox; it was his favorite. Many a night ended with them singing it, arm in arm, drunk as skunks. They vowed to meet up in the afterlife, in Margaritaville, should anything ever happen to one of them on the job. Swaggs died two days before his thirtieth birthday while trying to rescue a boy drowning in the Mad River. He left behind a wife and four children.

King passes through a security door to the main office, which is crammed wall to wall with battleship-gray metal desks piled high with case files. Manning the desks is a corps of loyal employees without whom the entire justice system would come to a halt. They are nearly always swamped with paperwork and rarely look up from their desks, but when King passes by on his way to Sharp's office, he is met with a host of sympathetic eyes. News travels fast in the close-knit world of police officers. He double checks to make sure his uniform is properly adjusted before knocking.

"Are you okay?" Sharp asks perfunctorily.

"Fine." King appears unfazed by the day's events.

Sharp looks up from the papers on his desk. "Have a seat, Adam."

"Thanks," King answers, "but I'd rather stand."

The patrolman has a hard time even standing still, restlessly shifting his weight back and forward on the balls of his feet.

"You are on administrative leave effective immediately," Sharp says.

The news hits King like a bucket of cold water.

"Until you're cleared by the brass."

"How long is that?"

"Hard to say," Sharp replies. "This is going to be a real media circus. Turns out the kid you shot was only seventeen. Remember the O'Kane case?" the lieutenant says, alluding to the controversial police shooting case from a few months earlier that was still fresh in the public's minds. The seventeen-year-old high school student was shot and killed by officers as he ran through the park with a knife. "So be prepared for the worst."

The thought of not riding his motorcycle for more than a couple of days *is* the worst thing he can imagine.

"I'll be holding your hand through the process," Sharp offers.

"Thank you, sir," King replies.

King knows he can trust the lieutenant. Sharp is a cop's cop.

"Follow me." The lieutenant gets up from his desk and motions with two fingers. The grim-faced superior leads King down the hall to the Public Information Office. He knocks lightly on the glass door, and the two enter.

Unlike the rest of the institutional decor in the department, the walls in the PIO are painted a cheery blue color. Karen Phillips, a buxom brunette in her thirties, welcomes them into her domain. Little does King know that she has had a thing for him ever since she saw him glide into the parking garage on his motorcycle. She was instantly drawn by the way he made it look so easy—not to mention the thousand-watt smile he flashed her after taking off his helmet. But he had no idea that Karen liked him in that way; she kept that secret to herself. Her career depended on maintaining a professional demeanor at the office, especially in the macho culture of the police force. "If there's only one thing you take away from this meeting," she began, "it's that you don't talk about the incident to anyone. Period. Is that clear?"

"Got it."

"Is . . . that . . . clear, Patrolman King?" Karen firmly repeats. "Anything you say can *and will* be taken out of context. Even a stray comment to a buddy can cost you your career."

King looks across the desk at her and notices her for the first time in a new way. His eyes are drawn to the voluptuous curves under her tight gray flannel skirt. He can't help but notice the outline of the sexy purple lace bra under her button-down shirt. Their eyes meet. The attraction between them is instantaneous and powerful.

"I think he's had enough of the riot act," Sharp says after noticing the silent exchange between Karen and King. "Let's go, Adam."

The lieutenant ushers the young patrolman out of the office, but then King returns to get his leather jacket, which he conveniently left on the chair. They awkwardly bump into each other while reaching for it. "Excuse me," King says, looking at her and smiling bashfully. The chemistry between them is palpable.

"That's all right," she says as she blushes. "I wish you'd done it sooner."

"Really?" the lieutenant says, cajoling King afterward in the hall. "The old 'I forgot my jacket' routine? I thought *I* was old school." Sharp smiles crookedly, which for him is the same as an outright laugh. Thirty years on the job wear heavy on his face. He counsels his young patrolman further back in his office. "Tomorrow's going to be a long day. You've got Dr. Weitzman in the morning and then the Review Board right after. So I want you to go home, eat a good meal, and pour yourself a stiff drink. Then have a nice long cry in the shower."

King isn't sure whether his superior is joking or not but follows his orders nearly to the letter. He shuts the door to his apartment, downs a few shots of tequila, and then reheats a two-day-old steak sandwich from the back of the fridge. He lives alone. The only sign of human contact is a faded photo on a kitchen shelf. It's an old picture of him with his ex-wife Victoria on the back of his old motorcycle. She is a stunning blonde with bright blue eyes and a beaming smile. Their marriage lasted four fun-filled years, until she took off with some rich guy from LA two years ago. "I'm tired of being a cop's wife," she had told him before leaving. King wonders where she is now as the salty sting of tequila hits the back of his throat.

King flops into the worn couch he'd gotten at the local bargain basement store. The lumpy seat cushions press into his back, but he ignores them. He just stares at his blank walls, trying to push the sight of that kid out of his mind. He feels tired, but no matter how he shifts his weight, the couch cushions manage to hit him in just the wrong spot. Exasperated, he gets up and heads for the bathroom, pausing at a rickety shelf that hangs on the wall. He glances from trophy to trophy. Most of them he'd earned on the motocross circuit, but the one on the end is a marksmanship trophy from his academy days. He stares at the little gold figure holding a pistol in the perfect firing stance. He tenses his jaw. Targets were clean; people are messy. A tidal wave of anger surges up from somewhere deep inside him, and he loses control. Sweeping the trophies from their lofty perch, he dashes them to the ground. Manically sorting through the bits, he picks out the little gunner figure. King hesitates for a moment and then crushes it into smithereens under his boot.

Recalling the lieutenant's advice, King seeks solace in the shower. Lingering under the hot water for almost an hour, he tries in vain to wash away the visual image of the shooting. The memory is permanently etched in his subconscious. Unable to cry, he feels only a dull sense of emptiness beyond tears. The patrolman wipes a clear patch in the steamy bathroom mirror and stares deeply. He doesn't recognize the face staring back. He sees the sunken expression and the deep wrinkles in his brow. His eyes have lost their sparkle. All he can see is the dull gaze of a killer.

CHAPTER TWO

KING WAKES TO THE SOUND of a stiff rap on his apartment door. The bleary-eyed patrolman stumbles out of bed and squints through the peephole. It's Lieutenant Sharp, looking crisp and morning fresh, holding two take-out coffees.

King opens the door. "Morning, sir."

"Let me guess—didn't get much sleep?" Sharp hands him a coffee. "In case you forgot, today's your appointment with the staff psychologist. Come on. I'm giving you a ride downtown."

King goes to get dressed. When he reemerges, the lieutenant is on his cell phone. "I'm en route."

"What's up?" King asks.

"A stabbing in the waterfront district," Sharp answers.

"We catch the guy?"

"No."

"Anybody we know?"

"They're running his prints now." Sharp shakes his head. "What is it about that neighborhood?"

High Speed Silence

*   *   *

When Sharp and King arrive at the station, they find that the antipolice demonstration has doubled in size. King can barely hear the siren above the din. Radical organizers have recruited busloads of agitators from outside of the area. King listens for a moment and hears their ringleaders droning "Child killer!" and "Double or nothing?" nonstop on their megaphones. He can't believe how badly they could distort the truth in such a short time. It pisses him off.

A small group of protesters dressed in Grim Reaper costumes whips up the crowd by waving their plastic scythes.

"So what are you going to be for Halloween?" Sharp jokes.

He is forced to push his way through the crowd with his bumper to get into the garage. He then escorts King to the elevator and pushes the button for the third floor. "Don't let him drive you crazy," he says, smiling crookedly, and then leaves abruptly. The young patrolman is grateful to the lieutenant for going the extra mile on his account. A lot of supervisors wouldn't do that. Or worse, they'd be throwing him to the wolves in order to cover the department's legal ass.

*   *   *

King hasn't been to the third floor of the headquarters since he took his psych test fresh out of the police academy. He remembers the ridiculous questions on the test, which seemed primarily focused on whether he liked flowers or not. "Here goes nothing," he says under his breath as he exits the elevator, bringing with him a healthy dose of skepticism.

Some people believe that everyone has a doppelganger, a virtual twin somewhere on earth. Dr. Isaac Weitzman looks like he could be Albert Einstein reincarnated. "Come, come," the bushy-haired staff psychologist beckons the patrolman into his office, which feels more like a private study. "I know you're not happy to be here," he begins, trying to put King at ease. "But statistics show that posttraumatic counseling is highly effective in helping police officers cope with the trauma of a shooting. I understand that you were involved in an *incident* yesterday?" Weitzman clicks his pen.

"Correct." King is tight lipped.

"Relax. You're not on the witness stand here."

"Sorry."

"Rough night?"

"Didn't sleep much," King says, still keeping his responses to a minimum.

"It's perfectly normal," the doctor reassures him. "It's one of the symptoms of shock. I can prescribe some medication, if you like?"

"Don't believe in the stuff," King says flatly.

"Interesting," the doctor says as he adds a check mark to King's file. "So," he says to indicate that he is getting to the matter at hand, "tell me what happened." King regurgitates his version of the story as if he were writing an arrest report.

"I see." Dr. Weitzman appears puzzled by King's seemingly detached attitude. "But more importantly, how are you *feeling* about all of this?"

"Just doing my job." King is beginning to feel like a broken record. He wonders how many more times someone is going to ask him how he *feels*.

"Surely you feel something? I mean, it's not every day that you violently end someone else's life."

"I didn't have much choice," King shrugs.

"Do you have any doubt that you took the right course of action?"

"Nope," King responds with absolute certainty. "It was textbook."

"Don't you regret that it happened?"

"I feel like shit that it happened!"

"That may seem like a small point"—Weitzman's tone turns serious—"but it's the doubt that can kill you. It can eat you up inside. Many police officers in your shoes try to bottle it up and end up as substance abusers or even *take their own lives*." The good doctor intones that this is the worst sort of tragedy. "If you ever feel *not right* about it, come see me. Okay?"

"Sure," King replies half-heartedly.

"Tell me, Adam," Weitzman says, taking a different tack. "Why do you like being a police officer?"

"My motorcycle," King responds unflinchingly. "When I'm on my bike, responding to a call, the world comes into focus. Everything . . . ," he says, in search of just the right words, "makes *sense*."

"Go on." Dr. Weitzman tries to draw King out of his shell.

"I hear the anarchy of the world through my headset every day," the patrolman explains. "It never stops; it just slows down sometimes. And when I'm lying awake at night, it plays on a continual loop in my head, like static. But when I roll on the throttle, it's like I'm outrunning all that madness. And just for a moment," King says, shutting his eyes, "everything just goes *silent*."

"Sort of a Zen thing?" Dr. Weitzman offers, trying to relate.

"I guess you could say that bike is my *source*. It separates me and takes me places no one else can go."

"I can see how important that must be in your line of work."

"And I've seen things you wouldn't believe."

"Like what?"

"The decapitated body of a seven-year-old girl," King states matter-of-factly. "The cell phone was still ringing in her pocket."

"That must have been terrible." The doctor cringes.

"Or the tortured hobble of a cat whose hind legs have just been run over." The patrolman reels off one horrible story after another. "And the odd bits of stuff I see in the median each day: weird photographs, clothing, and the endless sea of plastic crap."

"You must have a few *funny* stories?" Weitzman says, hoping to lighten the mood.

"Like the time I joined the Motorcycle Stunt Team," King relates. "In my very first show, they had me do this move where you lock the handlebars and then slide backward off the bike until you are hanging onto the sissy bar with your hands and dragging your feet in the dirt behind you. I performed the move all right," the patrolman amusedly recalls, "but they never showed me how to *crawl back up*! I went around the ring ten times before I was finally able to pull myself back on. And the crowd never knew. They thought it was all part of the act."

"Maybe you'll take me for a ride sometime?" the doctor jokes.

"It's not all fun and games, though," King continues. "Four out of the five guys on the team were dead before the age of thirty. One guy was killed in a traffic jam by a car passenger who deliberately opened his door as the officer passed by at sixty miles an hour. He sailed a hundred feet before hitting a utility pole headfirst. Another one used to race his bike to work, back when they let us take our bikes home. He slid under the back of a garbage truck when its driver slammed on the brakes."

"The third?"

"Uh," King says, swallowing hard. "I don't like to talk about that one."

"Why not?"

"Because it doesn't change a goddamned thing." King's voice wavers.

"Are you talking about your friend Swaggs?"

King is jolted by the sound of his dead partner's name. He doesn't like the way Weitzman brought it up. *He's not even a cop,* King thought. *How the hell could he understand?*

"It's okay, Adam," the doctor says in a softened tone. "I'm not going to pry. I just want you to realize that there may be some unresolved feelings there."

"Look, Doc," King replies. "If I stopped to think about my feelings all the time, then there's no way I could function each day. That goes with the job."

"Is that all you are, Adam? The job?" the doctor pauses. "What about your family life?"

King is caught off guard by the question and completely stymied. Weitzman has obviously read his file. It feels as if the doctor has neatly dissected him in a laboratory.

"What about it?"

"All I'm saying is that the two most important people in your life are gone, and they're never coming back. Until you come to terms with the sorrow, you'll never get ahead of it,"—the doctor pauses to let the thought sink in—"no matter how fast you ride that motorcycle."

"I see your point," King responds. Despite the fact that Weitzman's approach made him mad, he had to admit that he was right.

"By the way, you never mentioned what happened to the fourth man on the team," the doctor says.

"He was broadsided by a car at a stop sign," King recalls. "The funny thing is that it happened when he was off duty. The not-so-funny thing is that his girlfriend was on the back of the bike. She died, and he ended up in a wheelchair, paralyzed from the neck down."

"That's brutal," the doctor says. "Where is he now?"

"Blew his brains out."

Lieutenant Sharp is waiting for King when he emerges from the session. "You've got the Review Board in exactly . . ." he says, checking his watch, "twenty-eight minutes. Better get your game face on." Sharp offers to buy him a coffee at the courthouse cafe downstairs. Settling into a corner table, the two men sip their coffees and take a break from reality, if only for a few minutes.

"At least he didn't ask me whether I liked flowers," King jokes.

"You've got to watch those shrinks," the lieutenant says. "Sometimes they unearth stuff that's better off left alone."

"Do you remember your first psych test?"

"Yeah," Sharp laughs. "I failed it."

"No shit?"

"That's right," Sharp says. He blows on the steaming black coffee he is drinking and then takes a sip. "But I appealed it—and won."

"And just look where you are today!"

They both laugh. It does King good to see the lieutenant loosen up for once. It lets him know he is still human.

"Now, let's get you ready for the firing squad," Sharp says. "They're going to pepper you with hundreds of questions about everything from lethal force to what you had for breakfast that day. And they're not going to cut you any slack. It's grandstanding, mostly," Sharp explains. "But make no mistake. The department *will* cut you loose if it means avoiding an expensive lawsuit."

"Thanks for the pep talk."

"Look, we all get put through the ringer at some point in our careers. Today just happens to be your lucky day."

*   *   *

Adam King's hearing with the Review Board is nothing short of legal torture. He sits motionless while his every action is scrutinized by the panel. He feels like a frog being dissected in seventh-grade biology class. One Internal Affairs officer seems particularly intent on raking King over the coals. Inspector Brian Dickman has made a name for himself and gotten his revenge on the world for his laughable surname by weeding out the rank and file with extraordinary relish. He is hated and feared by officers on the street.

"How utterly irresponsible!" the bald, squatty inspector barks. He gets right in King's face, so close that King can smell the tuna sandwich he had for lunch. "'Double or nothing?' What *were* you thinking, Officer King?"

"He gave up, didn't he?" King replies.

"That's not the point!" Dickman snaps. "The use of that phrase constitutes a challenge, and that's not what they taught you in the academy. Is it, Officer King?"

King senses that the inspector is trying to wrap him up in a neat little ball so they can boot him out the door.

"What would you have done?"

"I'd have followed the *letter of the law!*"

"Hell," a board member in a white cowboy hat chimes in. "I kind of like it. It has sort of a Clint Eastwood ring to it."

"This community will not tolerate a Wild West mentality in its law enforcement officers!" Dickman continues. "For God's sake, the victim was only *seventeen years old*!"

As the inquiry drags on, King realizes that no matter what he says, he's screwed. So he falls back on the same robotic response to every question for the rest of the hearing: "I was just doing my job."

*   *   *

King stumbles out of the hearing feeling thoroughly worked over. He loosens his tie and heads to the men's room. The harried patrolman splashes some cold water on his face in the sink and takes a couple of deep breaths to unwind. "That sucked," he says to himself.

Exiting the washroom, King runs into Lieutenant Sharp, who is waiting for him. Sharp has a grim expression on his face. "I'm afraid I have some bad news," he says, hesitating. "It's about your friend Johnny."

"What now?"

"He's been stabbed."

CHAPTER THREE

HUMBOLDT CITY'S PRIMARY EMERGENCY ROOM is located at the Mother Mercy Hospital on the east side of town. King has been here too many times to count. Normally he maintains a professional detachment when he walks through its doors, but today, it's personal. He's known Johnny since way back when. They grew up in the same neighborhood together.

"Thank God you're here!" cries Johnny's mother, Nanette, a petite, graying blonde. She greets him like her own son. "Oh, Adam . . ." she says as she hugs him tightly.

"How's Johnny?" King asks.

"The doctors say he'll probably linger for a few days," she explains, her eyes welling up. "But eventually we'll have to make the decision."

They look at each other in silent agreement that Johnny wouldn't have wanted to go on this way. King buckles slightly and has to steady himself by putting his hands on his knees. He inhales and exhales deeply a couple of times and then regains his composure. *I've got to think about Nanette right now*, he thinks. "What happened?" he asks.

"Somebody found him in a crack house down at the waterfront. He'd been laying there for *two days*! I just don't understand it," she says, befuddled. "He'd gotten off the drugs and was going to school. I think he was even patching things up with his girlfriend."

"I see it all the time," King says. "The pull of the old lifestyle is so strong that it outweighs everything else."

"What else could I have done, Adam?" she asks pitifully.

"It's not your fault. Johnny has always been battling his own demons."

"But he's . . . *my world*."

"He's going to pull through this." King clasps her shoulders firmly and musters his best white lie. He says good-bye to Johnny's mom and heads straight out the door. He's in such a hurry that he doesn't even notice the front page headline at the newsstand. It reads: "DOUBLE OR NOTHING?"

"Sorry about your friend," says Lieutenant Sharp, who has been waiting outside by the curb for King.

"Then help me catch the *fucker* who did this!" King says, smoldering.

"Not so fast." Sharp can see that the patrolman is hungry for revenge. "You're on administrative leave, remember?"

"So what am I supposed to do? Sit around with my thumb up my ass?"

"Detective Mundy has been assigned to the case."

This is the first piece of good news that the patrolman has gotten all week. Mundy is a highly decorated veteran who always gets his man. "He'll probably want to *interview* you for possible leads . . ." Sharp says, hinting that King can aide the investigation without being directly involved. "Let's head over to his office."

*   *   *

As King heads to Detective Frank Mundy's office, he is not sure what to expect. Mundy is known around the department as a bit of a kook. He thinks outside the box, a glaring contradiction in the highly regimented law enforcement world. No one can argue with his results, though. He has the highest closure rate in department history. Those who work with him closely consider the senior detective an intuitive genius.

"Don't let his appearance fool you," Lieutenant Sharp warns King. "There's a method to his madness."

When King enters Mundy's office, he immediately realizes what Sharp was talking about. The first thing he notices is a rubber dummy head mounted on the wall. The placard below it reads: "The one that got away." The office is a total mess. Case files and odd bits of evidence are piled everywhere. There is a large, silver bowl full of pistachio nuts on the desk and a ring of discarded shells on the floor. "Just a second," Mundy says. The graying Irish detective continues staring at the file for what seems like an eternity. His twinkling blue eyes are fixed, and he appears to be in some kind of a trance. King remains standing motionless, like a good soldier. Finally, something clicks in the detective's head. "Aha!" He slaps his knee and then immediately picks up the phone. "That's right," he tells the person on the line. "Bobby Beck is definitely our man."

Mundy hangs up and then turns his attention to King. "A graffiti case," he explains.

"Oh, yeah?" King asks.

The detective picks up the file he had just been studying, which contains dozens of tagging photos. Some of the tags were found in the most amazing, and costly, locations around the city. He points out how Beck's *K*'s were always written in capital and leaned to the right. "Beck knew he was in for some serious time if we caught him, so he changed his moniker—but forgot about the *K*'s!"

"Nice catch."

"So," Mundy says as he finally turns to greet him. "You're the Evel Knievel we've been hearing so much about?"

"Yes, sir," King answers stiffly.

"Drop the 'sir' crap," the detective corrects him. "It's just Mundy. Now tell me about your friend Johnny."

Everyone in the department knows about King's repeated efforts to save his childhood pal from the ravages of heroine addiction. "It all started when he was a kid," King explains. "His back was broken in a car accident, and the doctors pumped him full of prescription meds. He was never quite the same."

"Do you think this current situation is drug related?"

"Probably."

"Who's his dealer?"

"That's the funny thing," King says, puzzled. "Johnny had cleaned himself up. His mother told me he was going back to school."

Mundy just shakes his head, having heard the same story so many times before. "I'm sorry about your friend, Adam."

King tenses his jaw. "I don't want your pity. I want you to get the guy who did this!"

"Because if I don't . . . you will?" The detective knows he has to handle King just right. A sawed-off cop eager for revenge can cause a lot of headaches. "Look, I think I can use you on this, but you have to play things my way. It's not just your ass that's on the line here. Capice?"

"Got it."

"Drug cases can get pretty squirrelly, and I might have to get creative. Folks in the Waterfront District are tight knit, and they don't like talking to cops. Are you willing to go undercover? And risk everything? Your job, your career, *your freedom*?" The detective knows the answer to that question before he even asks it.

King nods.

"Come on." He leads King to an adjacent squad room. "I'll introduce you to the team."

Mundy pulls a bird caller from his pocket, blows it twice loudly, and then repeats. "That's the call of the raven," he explains between *ca-caw*s. "It's the most intelligent of all birds."

A group of the weariest looking men on earth assembles at the worn metal briefing table. Their rumpled clothes, beard stubble, and bloodshot eyes indicate that they haven't slept in days. The bird call definitely got their attention.

"This is Patrolman Adam King . . . the one on *administrative leave*." Mundy uses hand quotations for comic emphasis.

"The 'double or nothing' guy?" someone in the squad asks. "Classic."

"Wish I'd thought of it myself," somebody else chimes in.

"The victim in the waterfront stabbing was a close personal friend of Officer King's." Mundy looks around the room at his men. He wants to light a fire under their collective backside. "Which means he's a friend of *ours*," he says in a Don Corleone voice, lightly touching both hands to his chest for effect.

A strikingly handsome black detective is the first to extend a hand and welcome King to the fold. "I'm Lamar Davis."

Davis is gracefully athletic and perfectly proportioned. He resembles a middleweight boxer. "And this is my partner, Detective Roddick."

King recognizes the name immediately. Roddick was an all-American track and football star at the state university. The blonde detective with the crew cut is Herculean in stature. He looks like he could wrestle a lion and win.

"Good thing he's on our side," King jokes.

"What've we got so far?" Mundy asks.

"Zilch," Roddick answers. "No witnesses, no prints, no nothing."

"Did you call the media with the tip line number and reward information?" Mundy asks.

"I'm on it," Roddick responds.

"How's our victim? I mean . . . Johnny." Mundy nods toward King as if to apologize for his bluntness.

"He's in a coma," King says bleakly. He looks down and catches himself as he says it. He had always wondered when this day would come for Johnny. Now the reality was upon him—upon them both.

"We leave no stone unturned!" Mundy exhorts his men as they wearily disperse.

"What about me?" King asks. "No way you're going to keep me on the sidelines."

"This is your last chance to play it safe," Mundy replies, "to just go home and let us handle it."

"Not on your life, Mundy." King's whole body tenses up. "I don't care if they *do* take away my badge. Johnny may not have been an angel, but he didn't deserve this. He never hurt a fly."

"Just wanted to make sure you were willing to go the distance," Mundy answers.

CHAPTER FOUR

THE *HUMBOLDT TATTLER* IS THE city's biggest newspaper. Its editors are decidedly antiestablishment. Police beat reporter Kurt Swyndall routinely fans the flames of public discontent by making the police look brutish and incompetent, and he's having a heyday with the Fourth of July incident. He knows it's a high-profile story and, quite possibly, his ticket to the big time. "I can't wait to get out of this godforsaken hellhole," he mutters to himself at the copy machine in his office. He is printing up flyers for a friend of his, one of the radical organizers of the courthouse demonstration. Technically, this is against newspaper policy, and it could get him fired. *Fuck it*, he thinks. *I'm getting out of this town one way or the other!*

The scrawny, shaggy-haired Stanford graduate with John Lennon-style spectacles never wanted to come to Humboldt City in the first place. He had applied for positions in all the major cities after college, but no one was hiring. The *Tattler* was the only newspaper that would pay him a regular salary. He figured it was as good a place as any to start, despite the fact that it served a small market. The weather was beautiful the weekend he came up for the interview, so he decided to take the job. And here he was, five years later, stuck in a city he hated. The weather was cold and foggy most of the time, and the people were mostly hicks. His acerbic articles didn't exactly endear him to the local population either. *Nobody appreciates my intellect up here*, Swyndall assures himself. *I'm just trying to enlighten them a little.*

He looks around to make sure no one is looking and then takes a quick glance at the flyer he has designed. It's a cartoon pig, depicting a motorcycle cop eating a strip of bacon. The caption below reads, "It's not murder . . . if the pigs do it!" "Very nice," Swyndall snickers. He hits the print button and runs off five hundred copies. Stuffing them into his messenger bag, the snooty reporter grabs his jacket and ducks out the door.

Swyndall also maintains an ongoing feud with the police department. He regards Karen Phillips as his nemesis and goes out of his way to be a thorn in her side. "She serves no other purpose than to obfuscate the truth and keep the public in the dark about the shooting," he'd written in his column that very morning.

*   *   *

"I'm so sick of this guy," Phillips says, slapping the morning *Tattler* down on the conference table at the weekly staff meeting. "It's bad enough that he picks on me; it's my job to be a target. But now he's going after Adam."

"Maybe Adam *should* be gone after," Inspector Dickman suggests.

"You mean sell him down the river?" Phillips responds.

"All I'm saying," the inspector begins, "is that it would take a lot of the heat off of the department."

"Back off, Dickman!" she snaps.

"Let's stay focused," Lieutenant Sharp says.

"I think I know how to handle this guy," Detective Mundy interjects.

"I'm listening," Phillips says.

"Why don't I grant him an in-depth interview?"

Phillips shakes her head. "Absolutely not. There's no telling how he'll twist your words to suit his ends. He'll end up making us all look like chumps. It's too risky."

"Come on. It'll be fun," Mundy says with a twinkle in his eye.

"It could lead to a break in the case," Sharp says.

"The only way I'd even consider it," Karen says, bending a little, "is if you stick to a prewritten script, with my prepared answers."

"What's that saying about keeping your friends close," Mundy says, grinning, "and your enemies even closer?"

The detective wants to play a little cat and mouse of his own.

* * *

Swyndall shows up at the police station at two-thirty that afternoon, thirty minutes early for his appointment. The overzealous reporter still isn't sure why he has been granted an interview, but the prospect of digging up dirt from within the department is irresistible. He has every intention of raking the police department over the coals in his column, and he's eager to get started. Detective Mundy watches Swyndall through the blinds in his office as he comes into the station. *Physically awkward, socially inept, probably got picked on a lot in the sandbox as a child*, Mundy figures. *Judging by the gold pinky ring and rumpled exterior, he comes from old money*. Mundy guessed that Swyndall never lived up to his daddy's expectations.

Swyndall saunters up like a fox in a henhouse. "Are you Detective Mundy?" he asks. There is a hint of condescension in his whiny voice.

"That'd be me," Mundy replies. The detective extends his hand for Swyndall to shake, but the reporter arrogantly ignores the gesture. "Look," Mundy leads off. "Maybe it's time the police and the press work together . . . in the best interests of the community?"

"Sounds to me like you're trying to hide something," Swyndall responds. "Did Karen Phillips tell you to say that?"

"What's the matter—afraid you might learn something?" Mundy replies.

Swyndall looks around the cluttered room with his nose in the air. He locks his eyes on Mundy's wall mount and twists his face into a cynical knot. "What's with the taxidermy?" he asks.

"My job can be rather depressing at times," Mundy explains. "So I try to lighten things up a bit."

"How moronic," Swyndall says.

"The department wants to give you a chance to see things from *our* perspective," Mundy says. "From the inside."

"And I have complete freedom to write whatever I want?"

"Absolutely."

"And no interference from Karen Phillips?"

"Wouldn't want it any other way. Pistachio?" Mundy offers the reporter the bowl full of nuts.

Swyndall turns up his nose. "So just how *does* your department plan on justifying the Fourth of July shooting?" he asks.

"Actually, it's a clear-cut case." The detective calmly hulls a pistachio and then nonchalantly tosses the shell on the floor. "The officer was fully justified in the eyes of the law."

"Just how do you figure?" Swyndall's tone is sarcastic.

"The standard distance at which police officers are trained to draw their firearms is twenty-one feet. The assailant was toe to toe with the officer, swinging a knife."

"Couldn't he have just run?"

"You mean *run away*?" Mundy is incredulous.

"Hey, if it would have saved a life . . ."

"But the officer *did* save a life."

"Oh, yeah?" Swyndall says irreverently. "Whose?"

"His own."

"Yeah, but that doesn't really count," Swyndall says.

"Oh, really?"

"You know what I meant," the reporter replies, trying to write off his comment.

"No, tell me. What *did* you mean?"

There is an uncomfortable pause in the conversation. Mundy just sits back in his chair and observes the reporter silently, cupping his chin with his hand. It has a very unnerving effect.

"What about pepper spray?" Swyndall quickly tries to change the subject.

"Pepper spray isn't particularly effective against people who have been subjected to it before," Mundy answers slowly. "Are you aware that the suspect had a lengthy criminal record, including convictions for drug dealing, weapons possession, *and* aggravated assault?"

"So in your eyes he's guilty until proven innocent, right?"

"No, but a person's criminal record is usually a pretty good indicator of his overall behavior. And this guy," the detective whispers as he leans in, "was *not* a nice guy."

"Sounds like the typical us-versus-them cop mentality," the reporter says.

"Actually," Mundy replies, "the majority of our officers are regular, middle-of-the-road people who are just doing their job."

"*Really*?" Swyndall says sarcastically.

"Don't get me wrong. There are a handful of assholes in every department. Not even their fellow officers like them. But they are the exception to the rule."

"You must be a big believer in *rules*?" The way Swyndall says this shows his complete disdain for authority.

"You have to draw the line *somewhere*," Mundy points out.

"At the point of a gun?"

"Sometimes."

"Face it," Swyndall says. "The system sucks."

"Sometimes," Mundy admits candidly. "But at least it tries to protect decent citizens from the shitbags of the world."

"Don't you mean dirtbags?"

"I mean the types that serve no real purpose on this earth other than to heap misery on everyone around them. And believe you me," the detective adds, "there's no shortage."

"Is that why you do it?" Swyndall says mockingly. "To punish the wicked?"

"Far from it," Mundy replies. "For me, it's all about happy endings."

"Happy endings?"

"In my profession, I am privileged to help people through some of the worst moments of their lives. Most of the time, nobody wins, even when we catch the bad guy. But every once in a while, some indescribable sort of universal fate intervenes on the side of justice, and the innocent get spared. That's why *I've* shown up to work every day for the past twenty years," Mundy says as he pokes his own chest. Mundy decides to turn the tables on the reporter. "Why do *you* do what you do?"

"Because I want the truth!" Swyndall responds self-righteously.

"In my experience," Mundy replies, cracking open a pistachio, "people only want as much of the truth as they think they can handle. The *whole* truth—now that's something else entirely." Mundy decides that it is time to introduce his new subject. "Speaking of which, there's one case in particular that you could maybe help us with," he says, "what with your special skills and all."

Swyndall sniffs haughtily. "What makes you think I want to help you?"

"I don't know, maybe something about—what was it—*the truth*?"

"What do *you* know about the truth?" Swyndall says with absolute contempt in his voice.

"I suppose you heard about the stabbing in the Waterfront District?"

"Nothing in Humboldt City gets by me."

"It's a complete dead-end so far," Mundy explains. "And even though you're untrained, you might stumble onto something by pure dumb luck."

"Are you sure this is legal?"

"Sometimes you have to give the law a little ... nudge," Mundy says with a wink. "Criminals don't usually walk into the station and just turn themselves in."

"That's reassuring, especially coming from a law enforcement officer."

"My job is to find out who did what," the detective states, "not pontificate on the finer points of the law."

"How *noble* of you," Swyndall says sarcastically.

Mundy scribbles his cell phone number on a piece of scratch paper and hands it to the reporter.

"What about—," Swyndall begins.

"Call me if you find out anything." The detective snubs him, abruptly terminating the interview.

Swyndall hustles out the door, eager to embarrass the police department by solving the case on his own. He is practically frothing at the mouth. This is his ticket out of this dump.

Detective Mundy waits until he is out of view and then assigns Detective Roddick to tail him. "Give him plenty of rope," the detective orders. "Maybe he'll lead us to the killer. Better yet," he adds, "maybe he'll end up hanging himself with his own words."

CHAPTER FIVE

WHEN THE SUN GOES DOWN on the Waterfront District, a different kind of folk crawl out from the woodwork. These are not day job people; many haven't seen daylight in weeks. They are the bottom of the barrel, cross-addicted to various substances, on top of being mentally ill to begin with.

Detective Frank Mundy is well acquainted with this decrepit cast of characters from his nights on the graveyard shift as a patrolman and in his current investigations. "One of the best ways to find out what's going on in this city," he always says, "is to chat up these people."

Mundy still likes to drive around at night in his aging Buick convertible with the top down wearing a loud Hawaiian shirt. "I miss the sounds and smells of the city," he explains. He looks more like a drunken golfer on holiday, and it helps him talk easily to these street urchins without blowing his cover.

One of the memory techniques he uses is dubbing them with descriptive nicknames for quick identification on the street. Lizard, for example, is a pock-faced heroin addict with bumpy skin and a darting green tongue. He hasn't brushed his teeth in years. The sight of his long, curled, funk-encrusted toenails has forced many a corrections officer to gag.

Prancy, on the other hand, is a perky hooker with a freshness of face that belies her long history in the trade. The nickname comes from the way she parades her wares on the avenue like a show pony in a miniskirt. She's also a valuable informant.

Mundy catches sight of her as he rounds the corner onto Fifth Street, where he pulls up to the curb.

Prancy struts over to his car, jiggling all the way. She's wearing a plaid miniskirt and an oxford shirt tied into a knot above the waist.

"Still wearing the schoolgirl number?" he says.

"Still wearing the same ugly neckties?" Prancy replies. When she leans over, Mundy gets a face full of her 44-DD fake boobs.

"Touché!" He appreciates the view. "So what else have you got for me?"

"Some nosy reporter came around earlier asking questions about that stabbing."

"I *think* I know the guy you're talking about."

"What a jerk!"

"He is kind of an ass," Mundy agrees. "Did you tell him anything?"

"No way I'm letting him cheat me out of that reward money!" she says. "So I just sent him down to the Buoy."

"You didn't!" The detective shakes his head, amused by the thought.

"Told him the folks down there might know something," she adds.

"Classic," Mundy said. "*Do* you know something, Prancy?"

"Yeah, but this one's going to cost you *extra*."

"I've got a friend who works the front desk at the Eureka Inn . . ." Mundy says. This isn't the first time he's dangled a free stay at the posh hotel under her nose.

"Throw in room service *and* a couple bottles of that fancy French champagne?"

"You drive a hard bargain," he says. The detective frowns, knowing that it's coming out of his own pocket. "Lay it on me, Mama."

"I heard from a john, who heard from some other guy, that the dude who got stabbed was with G. I. Joe right before it happened. And they were running from somebody."

Mundy is familiar with the vagrant whose trademark garb consists of military fatigues and a red beret. He's a permanent fixture on the waterfront, and trouble seems to follow him wherever he goes.

"Any idea who?"

"Now if I knew that," Prancy responds, "I would've held out for the honeymoon suite."

"Where does G. I. Joe hang out these days?"

"Most days he's in the food line over at the homeless shelter."

"Thanks, babe," Mundy says. "And next time, I want to see that leopard miniskirt outfit. You know it's my favorite."

"Just don't forget the champagne!" Prancy replies. She struts off, triumphantly shaking her ass. The clack of her cheap high heels echoes off the cobblestone.

*   *   *

Kurt Swyndall is openly nervous as he approaches the seedy waterfront bar called the Buoy. The reporter knows it's a haven for criminals and drug dealers. It is mentioned often in Karen Phillips's press releases. He stops on the sidewalk to wipe his brow and summon his courage. "If you want the big story, you've got to go where the story is," he tells himself.

The square, single-story watering hole is a throwback to frontier times. It looks like an old western saloon, except that it's painted bright aqua. It stands out like a sore thumb. The windows are painted black, and bars cover them. Except for a few neon beer signs, there is no sign of life from the outside.

Swyndall takes one last deep breath and then enters. It's dark inside—so dark that he has to squint to see anything. The last vestiges of light disappear as the door shuts behind him. He looks around the room and immediately feels out of place.

The first thing that catches his attention is the nude dancer on the bar top. She looks like she's pushing sixty and is missing her two front teeth. And she's giving the men at the bar more than an eyeful. She has perfected the fine art of blowing ping-pong balls out of her twat and into beer glasses.

Everyone in the joint looks scary, from the parolees at the pool table to the biker gang in the back. The beefy bartender eyes the young reporter suspiciously as he slides onto a barstool.

"What'll it be?" he asks.

"Got any white wine?"

"White wine?"

"Maybe a chardonnay?"

"Hey, boys!" the bartender hollers loudly. "The college boy here wants a chardonnay!"

Everyone in the bar laughs at Swyndall. There are a few catcalls, with threatening comments mixed in. The bartender pulls a cheap beer from the draft and plunks it down in front of the reporter. It's half foam. "That'll be eight bucks," he says.

"Eight bucks!"

"That's right. Eight bucks."

"I can buy a whole six pack for—"

"Next time," the bartender says, cutting him off. "Right now, you owe me eight bucks." The bartender points his thick, scarred finger right in Swyndall's face to make his point.

"Okay, okay," Swyndall says, coughing up the money. The bartender swipes it from his hand. Before he even gets a sip, a ping-pong ball lands in his mug. Disgusting. The fraternity pranks he pulled back at Stanford were one thing, but this is totally nasty.

"Chug! Chug! Chug!" the crowd shouts. They all turn, expecting him to take the next step. The dancer stands over him, impatiently checking her fingernails.

"Well, honey?" she says. "Why do you think it cost eight bucks?"

*   *   *

Detective Roddick shakes his head when he sees Swyndall enter the Buoy. He knows the kind of trouble the reporter will find himself in if he starts asking the wrong kinds of questions. The six-foot four-inch detective follows Swyndall into the bar as inconspicuously as he can. His entrance is not lost on the clientele. A surreptitious nod from the bartender alerts them to his presence. No doubt they immediately peg him as a cop. He slides into a booth near the door and puts his back against the wall. From there, he has an unobstructed view of the whole bar. He can't believe what he sees next.

Oblivious to criminal society etiquette, Swyndall starts asking questions about the stabbing. Nobody says a word. The men sitting next to him at the bar move away. Summoning his inner courage, the nervous reporter takes his beer and approaches the biker gang in the back. "Hi, guys," he blurts.

The bar goes silent.

"I heard you guys were cool."

"Fuck off."

"I'm a journalist," Swyndall explains. "And I'm doing a story on the biker lifestyle."

"We've got nothing to say to you," sneers Murdock, the club's menacing leader. He is the prototypical outlaw biker, clad in black leather from head to toe. He has a long black beard cinched with a rubber band, and he sports a black gambler's hat.

"I was hoping to hang out with you guys and tell your story in your own words."

"You're a nosy mother fucker, aren't you?" Murdock replies.

"I'll make you guys look really good . . ." the reporter adds.

"In case you haven't noticed, the *heat* is in the house." Murdock glances knowingly at Roddick. Swyndall clumsily turns around and spots the detective, who is trying to blend in. "Maybe we can go someplace where we can talk more freely?"

"Let's give him the slip," Swyndall says.

"Meet us at the fishing pier in a couple of minutes," Murdock suggests, "and you'll find out everything you need to know."

*   *   *

Swyndall pretends to use the bathroom and then sneaks out the back. When he gets to the pier, Murdock and his crew are already there, waiting for him.

"You really want to know what it's it like being an outlaw biker?" Murdock asks. "It's the ultimate form of freedom. But the lifestyle isn't for everybody; you have to be a *real man*." He pokes the scrawny reporter in the chest, implying that he doesn't qualify.

"So you must get a ton of chicks?" Swyndall asks.

"More than I can count," Murdock boasts.

"And there's probably nothing that goes on in this town that you don't know about first."

"Damn right!"

"Like, for instance . . ." the reporter hems, "the guy that got stabbed in the abandoned house?"

Wrong question.

"You're working with the cops!" Murdock growls.

"No!" Swyndall replies. "I fucking hate cops!"

"You're lying!" Murdock says. He rips open the reporter's shirt to check for a wire.

The severity of the situation finally dawns on Swyndall, who promptly soils his khakis. He hopes the gang won't notice it, but the hot stream trickles down his leg and onto the wooden planks. They erupt in laughter. "Look what we got here," Murdock announces. "A leaker!" Swyndall turns red; he has never been so humiliated in his life. The bikers knock him to the ground, rub his face in his own urine, and then begin stomping on him with their heavy leather boots. Murdock circles the fray like an alpha hyena.

"Please, no!" Swyndall cries. He suddenly realizes that he's in real trouble. He can't smart talk his way out of it this time.

Just as the outlaws reach for their knives, a bullet whizzes past and strikes a wooden pylon. "Hold it right there!" Detective Roddick's deep voice booms from the end of the pier. "You all are under arrest."

The former linebacker lines the bikers up at gunpoint and cuffs them to a handrail with plastic zip-ties. One of the gang members tries to ditch his knife by casually dropping it over the edge and into the bay.

"Unfortunately for you," Roddick says as he spots the big, shiny knife lying on top of the mud, "it's low tide."

"I bet you're not so tough without the badge and gun!" Murdock yells.

The Herculean detective promptly stiff-arms him off the pier and into the muck below. "Touchdown," he says with a broad smile.

Detective Roddick kneels down to check on Swyndall, who is curled up in the fetal position. Tears are streaming down his face. "You okay?" Roddick says.

"They were going to *kill* me!" Swyndall moans.

"Ya think?"

CHAPTER SIX

THE FOLLOWING MORNING, DETECTIVE LAMAR Davis is zeroing in on G. I. Joe. He stops by the homeless shelter at lunchtime, but there's no sign of him. No one in the chow line claims to know him. "Typical," Davis mutters to himself.

The detective returns to his unmarked car and parks a block away. He has a perfect vantage point of the homeless shelter. He surfs the Internet on his cell phone while he waits. Davis's wife has put him in charge of planning the family vacation. *Maybe Florida*, he thinks. *Definitely somewhere sunny*.

Thirty minutes later, the suspect saunters down the block. Davis waits and watches as G. I. Joe lines up for his free meal. He sees Joe's buddies warning him about the detective.

"Figures," Davis mutters. He jumps out of his car, crosses the street, and walks up right behind G. I. Joe. The old bird never sees him coming.

"What's up, Joe?"

The startled vagabond bolts immediately, running surprisingly fast for a scrawny old guy. "Go on, Joe!" his chow line buddies cheer him on as he makes his getaway. Unfortunately for him, Davis is the fastest man on the Humboldt City Police Force. The fleet-footed detective takes off after him, seamlessly informing dispatch on his handheld radio that he is "on foot pursuit" as he runs.

The chase that ensues closely resembles a fox hunt, with Davis as the hound. The wily fugitive darts through the back alleys of the Waterfront District, employing every nook and cranny to full advantage. Davis catches glimpses of Joe's red beret, always just out of reach, rounding corners. Other times, his quarry stands completely still, hidden in the shadows, as Davis passes right by him. But the seasoned detective knows every square inch of the waterfront and eventually manages to corner G. I. Joe in the building where Johnny was stabbed. Circling to the alley around back, he intercepts the elusive ragamuffin lowering himself out of the ground-floor bathroom window. He slaps the cuffs on G. I. Joe and clicks them extra tight. "Fancy meeting you here," he says.

Without warning, the old bird takes off again. This time he doesn't get far. Davis closes in on him like a missile. He tackles G. I. Joe cleanly, sending him into a patch of weeds.

"I didn't do anything!" the old bird yells. Dirt covers his face.

"Never said you did," Davis replies. The detective gets up, dusts off both knees, and readjusts himself. "But the fact that you ran means you're probably guilty of something."

High Speed Silence

"*Probably* isn't the same as *beyond a reasonable doubt*," G. I. Joe squawks. "I know my rights!"

Davis responds by yanking him to his feet and shoving him into the back seat of his car. "How about the *right to remain silent?*" he asks and then slams the car door shut.

CHAPTER SEVEN

BACK AT THE STATION, MUNDY congratulates Swyndall on the arrest of the bikers. Mundy has decided that it is best to coddle him a bit. After all, Swyndall knows that Mundy's getting the reporter involved in the investigation was blatantly illegal.

Mundy pats him on the back. "Attaboy!"

"Ow, not so hard!" The battered journalist is still in a state of shock. He is shaking uncontrollably and winces in pain every time he moves.

"We deal with guys like that every day," Mundy tells him. "That's why we carry guns."

"Maybe *I* should start carrying one."

"You're starting to sound like one of us."

"Heaven forbid," the reporter replies. He cracks a smile, and Mundy knows he's going to be all right.

"How'd you like to watch us interrogate one of them?" the detective asks.

High Speed Silence

Mundy ushers Swyndall into an observation room so he can get a close-up view. "Enjoy the show," he says before exiting. The interrogation room is little more than an empty office with only a gray steel desk with a sturdy metal rail along one edge. Murdock is handcuffed to the rail, sitting in a metal chair. He appears smaller and less threatening in this setting but still gives off a powerfully evil vibe. He stares intently at the one-way mirror, never flinching, with a hate-filled expression.

Mundy enters the room, knowing fully that Murdock isn't going to talk. "So what's your story?" he asks.

"Go fuck yourself, cop."

"I'm not as flexible as I used to be," Mundy replies. "Maybe you can demonstrate?"

"I want my lawyer," Murdock responds. There is a flicker of anger in his eyes.

"Bummer. I was prepared to offer you a deal."

"Law-yer!"

"The kind of deal that lets you walk out of here today. Look," Mundy says, "all I want is some information."

"About what?" Murdock growls.

"About the stabbing in the Waterfront District this week."

The stone-faced biker ignores the question and glares at the mirror as though he can see right through it.

"Otherwise," Mundy continues, "I'll have to charge your boy with possession of a concealed deadly weapon with intent to do grave bodily injury. That's some serious time he's looking at."

"He's not my problem," Murdock replies.

"Some club leader you are."

"What goes on in my club is none of your business."

"What do you think he'll say when I tell him?"

"He knows the score."

"He'll never talk, right?"

Mundy stops to let the thought sink in. "Okay," he then announces. "You're free to go."

The senior detective exits the room and rejoins Swyndall in the observation room.

"Are you crazy?" Swyndall asks.

"I didn't have anything to hold him on," Mundy says.

"But they tried to kill me!" The despondent reporter can barely get the words out. He can't believe what he just witnessed.

"It's better this way," Mundy explains.

"Better?"

"That's right—better. Murdock is involved somehow, but I need to find out how."

"How do you know?" the reporter asks.

"It's not something they teach you at the academy," Mundy explains. "It's the way a person reacts when posed with a direct question. Some guys are better at hiding it, but I've been lied to so many times that I can smell it. And by the way," he adds, pointing at Murdock, "he can't really see through the glass; he's just trying to mind-fuck you."

*   *   *

Meanwhile, Detective Davis is busy interviewing G. I. Joe in another room. "So your real name is Frank Lee,"

Davis says, scanning the old bird's rap sheet. "And what's this? You're currently on parole with *two strikes*?"

"They won't revoke me just for running away!"

"If you've got nothing to hide," Davis replies, "then why did you run?"

"I've got two strikes, man!"

The futility of interrogating a hard-core junkie is not lost on Davis, so he gets straight to the point. "Look, we've got a witness that puts you at a stabbing."

"I don't know nothing about no stabbing!"

From behind the one-way glass, Frank Mundy's finely honed instincts detect something in the old man's body language. "I'll take it from here," he says as he enters the room and excuses Davis. "And can you bring a soda for Mr. Lee?"

"Oh, I get it," the old bird says. "It's the *good cop's* turn."

"Come off it," Mundy says, employing a little verbal judo. "You and I both know there *are* no good cops."

The veteran detective is a virtuoso in the art of interrogation. Swyndall watches in awe as Mundy deftly plays the suspect like a pawn shop fiddle. "So your first name is Frank? Mine too."

"You're giving me a bad name." The old bird cackles at his own joke.

"So can I be *frank* with you?" the detective says, topping him. "We know you were involved in a stabbing down at the waterfront a few days ago. What can you tell me about it?"

"What stabbing?" G. I. Joe replies, trying to play dumb.

"Do you know a man named Johnny?"

"Johnny who?"

"We have a witness who puts you with him right before it happened," Mundy replies. "That makes *you* our number one suspect."

"I didn't stab nobody!"

"Then who did?"

"How the hell should I know?"

"I'm going to have to charge you with it."

"Then I want a lawyer." The felon is well versed on his rights. He's been interrogated too many times to count.

*   *   *

Walter, the public defender, shows up within the hour. He looks overworked. His bargain basement suit is wrinkled, and he has a five o'clock shadow. "Hello, Frank," he says.

"Hello, Walter," Mundy replies.

"What have you got for me this time?"

"Oh, you're going to love this one."

"Don't I always?"

The lanky attorney with salt and pepper hair enters the interrogation room and plops his brown leather briefcase on the table. Like its owner, the case is worn and second-rate to begin with. It's the best he can do on a civil salary. Mundy gives them a few moments to confer and then knocks on the door and enters the room.

"*Really*, Frank?" the public defender says. "This just might be your most harebrained work yet."

"Is that so?"

"You've got no eyewitnesses, no forensic evidence, and no confession. Am I missing something here?"

"True," Mundy admits. "But I *can* charge your client with a lesser offense and *still* deal him his third strike."

"For running from the police?"

"I'm talking about burglary."

"Burglary?" the public defender and G. I. Joe reply in unison.

"During the foot chase, your client illegally entered a dwelling with the intent to commit another crime," Mundy asserts. "If you check the penal code, the elements are all right there."

"What other crime?"

The public defender and G. I. Joe wait with bated breath to hear Mundy's answer.

"Evading a police officer," Mundy says. He smiles like the cat that swallowed the canary. He knows it's a ridiculous stretch.

"You're trying to pull a rabbit out of a hat," the public defender replies. Despite his objections, he is both shocked and impressed by the detective's manipulative interpretation of the statutes.

"I'm a man who wears many hats."

"It'll never stick."

"That's what they said about crazy glue."

"Then we'll see you in court."

"Walter, Walter," the detective says, seamlessly switching gears. He puts a hand on the attorney's shoulder and softens his tone. "Don't we always make nice in the end?"

The public defender hesitantly nods yes.

"Look, we know that he didn't stab anyone," Mundy continues. "We just want to find out who did. If he can tell us that," the detective says, "then your client walks. Now. Today."

"Give me a minute?" the public defender replies. He confers with G. I. Joe, and after a long discussion he persuades the old bird to talk.

"It was a dealer," G. I. Joe offers.

"Does this dealer have a name?" Mundy replies.

G. I. Joe looks at him like he's crazy. "I never asked."

"What does he look like?"

"A rough-looking white dude, with his underwear hanging out of his pants like the rest of those fools," Joe answers. "Always wears a belt buckle knife."

"Who's he work for?"

"Some biker dude."

"That's it?" Mundy presses. "You don't know his name or anything?"

"I think it was Mel, or Mal . . . or something like that."

"Would you recognize a photo of him?"

"Guess so."

*   *   *

On the other side of the glass, the astonished reporter can't believe how artfully Mundy has managed to pry the information out of the suspect. "Not my best work," the detective says to the reporter in his office afterward. "But it'll do."

Once again, he offers Swyndall a handful of pistachios. This time, Swyndall accepts. "Don't mind if I do," he says. He cracks one open and chomps it between his teeth. "What do I do with the—"

"Just toss it on the floor," Mundy says, discarding a nutshell of his own.

The reporter follows suit, adding his own empty shell to the heap.

CHAPTER EIGHT

■■■■■■■■■

DETECTIVE FRANK MUNDY WASTES NO time following the lead coughed up by G. I. Joe. Something is nagging him. He instructs Detective Davis to compile a photo lineup of past suspects named Mel or Mal, including one very special entry.

"Do you recognize anyone?" Mundy asks, placing the photo lineup and a red pen on the table in front of the junkie.

"That's him right there!" G. I. Joe exclaims.

"Are you sure?" Mundy asks.

"Sure, I'm sure!"

The old bird grabs the pen and circles one of the mug shots.

"Abracadabra!" Mundy remarks. He picks up the photo sheet like a magician pulling a rabbit out of a hat and holds it up so that Swyndall and Davis can see.

Their jaws drop. Circled in bright red ink is the mug shot of Malforth Allard Jr., the very same man whom Patrolman Adam King shot on the freeway.

"Looks like Allard stabbed Johnny the day *before* he got shot," Mundy concludes. He isn't overly surprised by the strange twist. Allard is a known drug dealer and Murdock's associate.

"Get forensics to confirm this right away," Sharp instructs. "Maybe Adam can get his life back now."

*   *   *

Meanwhile, administrative leave is taking its toll on Adam King. He paces back and forth in his apartment, climbing the walls. He can't even watch television to kill the time; nonstop coverage of the July Fourth shooting is on every channel. The patrolman is vilified by picketers who are shown carrying "Child killer!" signs.

"Is he *ever* going to call?" King asks himself. "I've got to get out of here." He finally decides to get some fresh air.

But as soon as he steps outside, King can hear the sound of the courthouse demonstration in the distance. It makes him feel like a stranger in his own neighborhood. When he stops for a soda at the corner market, the usually friendly Russian owner shoots him a dirty look.

"Why you have to shoot a boy?" he says in broken English.

"How much for the tequila?" King replies.

"Ten ninety-five."

The owner grabs a pint bottle from the shelf, stuffs it into a small brown paper bag, and hands it to King. "That is why I left my country!"

Returning to his empty apartment, a profound sadness settles over the patrolman. There is nothing left to do but sit, drink tequila, and stew in his own juices. Peering through the curtains at the gloomy fog, the patrolman feels trapped. In a drunken stupor, his thoughts turn to suicide. "It would be so easy," he tells himself.

King clumsily pulls his off-duty weapon from its black leather holster, a .40 caliber mini-Glock, and stares down the barrel. "Besides, nobody would really miss a motorcycle cop."

Physically exhausted, emotionally drained, and stinking drunk, the beleaguered patrolman finally reaches the end of his rope. Without further ado, he puts the muzzle in his mouth and pulls the trigger.

CHAPTER NINE

KING'S CELL PHONE VIBRATES ON the coffee table in his apartment, and then the call goes to voice mail. His limp body lays across the armchair next to it, the gun on the floor near his outstretched hand. The apartment is completely silent.

A few seconds later, King's eyes pop open, and he realizes that he had passed out. The first thing he sees is the gun on the floor. Picking it up, he finds nine rounds in the magazine and one jammed in the chamber. "Well, fuck me!" He laughs at his own stupid luck. He ejects the bullet and sets it upright on the coffee table. Its shiny brass jacket glints in the morning sun.

King hears his phone beeping, so he checks his voice mail. He recognizes the number; it's a message from Mundy.

"I think we know who killed Johnny," it says. "But we need to check out one last lead first. Are you ready for that little assignment? Call me."

He quickly calls the detective back.

"Put on some kind of disguise, and then go down to the Buoy," Mundy instructs him. "Ask for a guy named Murdock. Tell him your name is Butch and that you're fresh out of lockup. I've got an informant at the jail who'll vouch for you."

"Got it."

"Then tell him that G. I. Joe cut some kind of deal and is back out on the street."

"What's that supposed to mean?" King asks.

"Don't worry about it," Mundy replies. "You'll know why soon enough."

King follows the detective's instructions to the letter. He puts on a beat-up leather jacket and wraps a blue bandana around his head. King puts on mirrored sunglasses and checks himself in the mirror. He looks like a Mafia construction worker. He is careful not to forget the mini-Glock, which he tucks into the waistband of his jeans. Good to go.

Stashed in the alley below is a street bike he keeps for personal use. It's a leftover from his motocross days, a little beat up but still quite capable. King pulls back the worn cover and admires the machine. It brings back a lot of memories. All the old scrapes and scuffs are still there, with a story behind each one. He gets on. The feeling of that old seat is good, broken in perfectly. King inserts the key and pushes the red start button, and the trusty 300 cc engine comes to life. It's not a big engine, nor a big bike, but it's lightweight, maneuverable, and perfectly balanced. In many ways, he likes it better than his police cruiser. It's not so cumbersome. With a smooth downstroke of his foot, he puts it in first, rolls back the throttle, and slowly lets out the clutch. It's just the way he remembered it, like an old friend. Rolling quietly down the alley, the patrolman feels like himself again. When he gets to the street, he guns the motor. The rush of instant speed floods his body like a drug. It feels good. It had only been a couple of days since he'd ridden, but it was like going through withdrawal. No wonder he was so mixed up. It's also strange for him to ride a motorcycle off duty. Drivers are all over him, crowding his lane and cutting him off. When he's on duty, no one comes within five car lengths of him. Not only that, but they miraculously discover their turn signals.

When he gets within a block of the Buoy, King slows down to remind himself why he is there. He also knows he must make a grand entrance. There's no way the bikers would take him seriously if he didn't. It's been a couple of years since he's done a wheelie. *Oh well,* he thinks. *This is for you, Johnny.*

King revs the motor a few times and then releases the clutch. He goes straight to second gear and pulls back hard on the handlebars. The front wheel pops up off the ground perfectly. It's nice to know some things never change. The patrolman zooms down the block and past the saloon, in full view of Murdock's lookouts, who are standing in the doorway. He disappears down the street, turns around, and zooms past again. This time he is standing upright on the seat with his arms outstretched like an eagle's wings. Whizzing past, he can see the burly bikers motioning to one another as if to say, "Holy shit! Did you see that?"

King knows he's made a good impression, so he pulls over and parks his bike by the curb. He is careful not to appear rushed or nervous. He doesn't want them making him out to be a cop.

"Nice riding," the first biker says. He is small and wiry, with stringy blond hair and a goatee.

"Thanks," King answers.

"What's that piece-of-shit bike you're riding?" asks the other, a big brute wearing an Oakland Raiders cap. His openly hostile tone indicates that it's not really a question.

"Heard I could get a cold beer here," King says. "And see some titty."

The two outlaws look him up and down and then step aside to let him enter. "You like ping-pong?" they ask.

King enters the seedy bar and sits down at a barstool. He orders a beer and keeps his head down, minding his own business. He knows that he's being watched. After a couple more beers, he feels relaxed enough to look around the room a little more, but he is still careful not to make eye contact with anyone. Finally, he slips the bartender a twenty and tells him that he has some information for Murdock. The bartender stares him down, takes the twenty, and says nothing. A few minutes later, a member of Murdock's club comes over and tells him the boss will see him now.

King heads to the back booth, where Murdock is hanging out with the club officers. It is dark and smoky, and it's difficult to see any faces. They are discussing some secret club business in hushed tones as King approaches. Two big, mean-looking club members frisk him and remove his pistol. "What's this?" Murdock asks.

"My insurance agent," King says. "Never know when you'll need him."

"A Glock," Murdock comments. "That's a cop's gun."

"Stolen," King replies.

"Better be. So who the fuck are you?"

"My name's Butch, and I have some information for you."

"What kind of information?"

"I just got out of county lockup, and a little bird told *me* to tell *you* that some guy named G. I. Joe made a deal with the pigs and is back out on the street . . . whatever that means."

Murdock's mood suddenly turns dark. "Call Chico at the jail," he tells one of his men. "Find out if this guy is for real."

King waits nervously as the call is made. He hopes Mundy has his back.

"Okay," Murdock finally says. "Looks like it checks out."

"Glad to be of service," King replies. "What's this all about anyway?"

"Normally, I don't discuss club matters with an outsider, but since you did me a solid, I'm going to trust you. *Can* I trust you, Butch?"

"Of course you can't trust me," King says. "I'm a fuckin' parolee!"

They both laugh.

"Let's just say that one of my guys got carried away," Murdock explains.

"Carried away?"

"Well, he kind of . . . took out the wrong guy. Some local dude, a junkie. G. I Joe's the only one who can connect me to it."

So there it is. King knows it's Johnny he's talking about. It's a hell of a way to find out that a friend was murdered for no good reason. He was simply in the wrong place at the wrong time.

"It's no big deal," Murdock adds. "I mean, who cares about some worthless junkie anyway?"

King is tempted to reach across the table and choke Murdock right then and there. It suddenly dawns on him why Mundy has sent him on this little errand. The detective wasn't following a lead; he was giving King the chance to take care of Murdock himself, in his own way. "Can I have my gun back?" he asks.

"Sure thing," Murdock says as he passes it to him. "You're welcome here anytime, Butch."

King gets up from the table and heads for the door. His heart feels like it's going to leap out of his chest. A terrible rage starts to well up inside him, and his body goes cold. The rational side of his brain begs him to walk out the door and turn things over to Mundy. His darker side tells him to turn around and put a bullet through Murdock's head. He decides to return to his barstool instead and figure out his next move.

A few beers later, fate intervenes. Murdock heads to the bathroom solo, and King senses a golden opportunity to confront him alone. After checking to make sure the coast is clear, he follows the club leader into the men's room. Murdock is standing at the urinal, taking care of business, when King enters.

"What's up, Butch?"

"Just draining the main vein."

King lines up at the urinal two spaces away and pretends to unzip. He waits until Murdock is finished and then pulls his gun. "You fucking cockroach!" he snarls, grabbing the biker by the lapel and jamming the muzzle in his nose.

"Easy, Butch!" Murdock says, his hands up in surrender. "Don't do anything crazy! You want money? I can get you money!"

"I don't want your stinking money, Murdock."

"Then what do you want?"

"I want justice!"

"Justice? For what?"

Murdock starts to sweat. He knows fate has caught up with him this time. "Who are you, *really*?" he asks.

"That junkie?" King says, shoving the barrel forcefully up Murdock's right nostril. "He was a friend of mine."

"Oh, shit!"

"His name," King says as he twists the barrel a little more, "is *Johnny*!"

King makes Murdock lie face down on the floor. The tiles are filthy and splattered with urine and pubic hairs. With one foot on the back of Murdock's neck, King pulls out his cell phone and dials Mundy for backup. "Come and get him," he tells the detective, "before I change my mind."

Suddenly, King feels a sharp thwack on the back of his head. He feels dizzy for a brief second and then drops to his knees. A thick stream of his own blood pours down his scalp and into his left eye, blinding him. The sharp sting feels like a knife wound. The vision in his right eye is blurry, almost nonexistent. He is so disoriented that he cannot even look up to see who Murdock's accomplice is. He can see only the thick leather boots of the biker who has just hit him with a lead pipe. King desperately feels around on the floor for his gun and finds it, but Murdock steps on his hand before he can grasp it.

"You lookin' for this?" Murdock twists the gun away from King and points it down at him.

King tries to move, but it feels like a thousand pounds of sand are on his back, holding him down.

"Kiss your ass good-bye, along with your punk friend!" Murdock yells.

King looks up through his blurry eye, watching helplessly as Murdock aims for his face and cocks the hammer.

BAM!

A loud crash comes from the barroom, interrupting Adam's execution. The saloon is being raided by Mundy's posse. They had been staked out in an empty office building across the street the whole time.

"Let's get the fuck outta here!" Murdock says to his pal.

King can barely make out the image of Murdock and his cohort as they escape through the window and ride off on their choppers. He can tell by the sound of their pipes that they are headed north on Fifth Street. A few seconds later, Detective Roddick finds him on the bathroom floor.

"We need medical!" Roddick shouts. "Officer down!"

"Cancel that!" King says angrily. "This isn't over."

Leaning on his friend for support, King struggles to his feet and wipes the blood out of his eye with his shirtsleeve.

"You all right?" Roddick asks.

"Never better," King utters as he staggers out the bathroom door. He stumbles through the bar, ignoring everyone, and heads for his motorcycle. "Fuck!" he says, fumbling for his keys. He knows that every second counts if he's going to catch Murdock. He finds them, starts up his bike, and peels out, tires smoking.

King turns the corner quickly and heads up Fifth Street at full throttle, running red lights along the way. "Gotta catch up before he reaches the Samoa Bridge!" he tells himself. He knows that once Murdock is over that bridge, he is home free. From that point, there are too many directions he can go in.

The patrolman knows every back alley and shortcut in the city, however, and uses this knowledge to shave down the distance between himself and Murdock. King takes a series of twists and turns and ends up right at the foot of the bridge as Murdock speeds past. King cuts across two lanes of traffic, narrowly avoids a dump truck, and pulls up right behind him. He is so close now that he can see Murdock's shocked expression in his side-view mirror.

With one blurry eye—the other stinging with blood—King chases his foe across the bridge at blinding speeds, and he's without a helmet. He's breaking all the rules, and it feels damn good. He senses a clearer purpose than he has ever felt before. It's as though a divine force is working through him. This is more than just a job and more than simply personal. It's flat-out good versus evil.

At the bottom of the bridge, Murdock makes the cardinal mistake of turning south toward the Samoa jetty. It's a dead-end.

"You're mine now!" King says to himself.

Murdock zooms ahead, ditches his motorcycle in a sand dune by the side of the road, and runs toward the rock jetty. King is a hundred yards behind him and gaining. Murdock spins and shoots at King as he runs, missing wildly. King chases him to the end of the jetty, where rough ocean waves pound the slippery, barnacle-encrusted rocks. There's nowhere else to go.

"Give it up, Murdock!" King yells.

"Don't come any closer!" Murdock snarls.

King advances despite the fact that Murdock has the gun pointed at him. Just as Murdock prepares to pull the trigger, a big wave breaks over the jetty wall and knocks him off his feet. He stumbles and falls into a crevasse below the waterline, breaking his ankle in the process.

"Help!" he cries as the rough saltwater swirls around him.

"I could just walk away," King says, looking down at him pitilessly, "and let the tide drown you. Nobody would ever know but you and me."

"Fuck you!" Murdock aims his gun at King from below and pulls the trigger, but the magazine is empty.

"It sucks to be you," King says.

King turns his back and walks away. He hears Murdock cursing and screaming for nearly fifty yards before the sound of the waves drowns out his ruckus.

King walks back to his motorcycle and starts to ride away, but the image of the Law Enforcement Code of Ethics on Detective Mundy's office wall flashes into his mind. "That Code is the only thing I've really got in this world," King realizes. "They can take away my badge . . . and even my bike . . . but they can't take that from me. Nobody can."

He pulls over and quickly calls Mundy on his cell phone.

"Just where the hell are you?" Mundy wants to know.

"I'm at the Samoa jetty."

"Is he . . . ?"

"No, he's alive," King answers.

"Attaboy!"

"Better send medical," he advises.

King waits for the cavalry to arrive and then directs them toward Murdock. "You can't miss him," he tells paramedics. "Just head out on the jetty, and you'll hear him soon enough."

Back at the station, Detective Mundy gathers his squad for debriefing. He invites them into his office and shuts the door. Lieutenant Sharp and Karen Phillips are also in attendance. "No one is to know that Adam was in on Murdock's arrest," he instructs. "No one but us."

All agree.

"How did you know I wouldn't kill Murdock?" King asks.

"Just a hunch," Mundy replies. "But I thought I owed it to you to find out for yourself."

"It's up to you to put the right kind of spin on this, Karen," Sharp adds. "Just make sure Swyndall doesn't get wind of it, or we'll have a full-scale riot on our hands."

"I think I can handle it," she replies.

"Thanks, Karen," Adam says.

"Maybe you can help me go over some of the details?"

"O-o-o-h-h!" the squad teases. "It's about time you made your move, Karen!"

"How did you—?" Phillips stutters.

"We're detectives, remember?" the group replies.

"Oh, shit," King says, looking at his watch. It's the day Johnny's mom is going to disconnect him from life support. He rushes out of the meeting and dashes over to the hospital, hoping he isn't too late.

Johnny's family is assembled in the intensive care unit when Adam arrives. "Thank you for coming," Johnny's mom says as she hugs him like she's never going to let him go. He notices the heavy, dark bags under her eyes. "You look terrible," he says.

"It was a long night," Nanette answers. "I lay awake all night in my bed asking the Lord if I'm doing the right thing. Do you think I'm doing the right thing, Adam?"

"Yes."

"Me, too," she whispers in his ear with a mixture of sorrow and relief.

"Are we ready?" the priest gently puts his hand on her shoulder and asks the impossible question.

"Ready," she says.

He accompanies her into the room where Johnny lays. Nanette sits down on the bed beside him and takes his hand.

"Thank you for being my son," she says. Her lips tremble as she says the words. "You are the light of my life and always will be."

King kneels down beside her and says good-bye to his childhood friend. "You've always been like a brother to me," he utters. He leans down to hug him good-bye. A single tear rolls from his eye and falls on Johnny's cheek. "We got 'em, buddy," he whispers. "We got 'em."

The others form a circle around Johnny while the doctor unplugs him from life support. "Lord," the priest says, beginning the last rites, "we deliver unto You your faithful servant."

Just as his name starts to roll off the priest's tongue, Johnny suddenly opens his eyes. "What are you guys doing here?" he says as he looks around in a daze.

Cheers, tears, and shrieks of joy spontaneously erupt from the group.

"It's a miracle!" the priest proclaims.

The doctor quickly examines Johnny's vitals signs. "Well, I'll be damned," he says, flabbergasted. "I've read about this in textbooks, but . . ."

"You must be an angel," Nanette says to King, tears streaming down her face. "Somehow, you're always there when we need you."

Lieutenant Sharp and Detective Mundy are waiting for Adam outside.

"Looks like you got some good news?" Mundy says.

"The best kind." King wipes a tear from his eye. "Johnny's alive!"

"Glad to hear it. Ready for some more good news?"

"What's that?"

"We've closed the case on Johnny's attacker," says the lieutenant.

"Well?" King asks. "Who was it?"

Sharp whispers the answer in King's ear. The shocked expression on King's face becomes the fondest memory of his career. "So that means . . ." Adam mutters in disbelief.

"I had a feeling that Murdock was connected to it," Mundy explains. "But I couldn't be sure. Not until he admitted it to you in the bar. Sorry I couldn't tell you before."

"And in light of our investigation," Sharp continues, "the Review Board will have no choice but to clear you. You'll be riding a desk for a couple of weeks, but then it's right back to patrol, where you belong."

King is dumbfounded.

"So it looks like you'll be needing *these* back," the lieutenant says as he dangles a set of motorcycle keys in front of King.

He doesn't have to say it twice. The patrolman snatches them out of his hand.

"Looks like a happy ending to me," Mundy concludes.

EPILOGUE

A COUPLE OF WEEKS LATER, King returns to active duty. On his first day back, he stops for coffee at a roadside joint on the outskirts of the city. Glancing at the newspaper rack behind the counter, he notices the headline in the morning *Tattler*. It reads: "Frank Lee, I Couldn't Have Done It Without You."

"And a morning paper," he says to the cashier while paying for his coffee. King goes out to the parking lot, sips his coffee, and reads the article.

Kurt Swyndall has written a shockingly pro-law enforcement piece, which details the ironic conclusion to the two interconnected cases. The reporter waxes poetic about the courage, honor, and dedication of police officers. He makes himself out to be a hero in the case, as though he practically solved it on his own. He wins a national award for the article and then moves to Los Angeles.

The courthouse demonstrators disperse just as fast as they appeared. Turns out the citizens of Humboldt City have little tolerance for violent criminals.

Finishing his coffee, Adam King chuckles to himself and then tosses the newspaper into the garbage can. He straddles his bike, starts it up, and picks up right where he left off. He knows he's where he belongs. Having been truly tested by fate, the patrolman no longer hears any static in his mind. Rolling on the throttle, he hears nothing but the sound of high speed silence.

APPENDIX

LAW ENFORCEMENT CODE OF ETHICS

As a law enforcement officer, my fundamental duty is to serve mankind; to safeguard lives and property; to protect the innocent against deception, the weak against oppression or intimidation, and the peaceful against violence or disorder; and to respect the Constitutional rights of all persons to liberty, equality, and justice.